I AM THE EAR[TH]

AND THE EARTH IS ME.

HANNA
GERLACH

I am as Strong as the Mountains,

I am as wise as the Trees,

and I am as Free as the Wind.

I am as selfless as
the Sun,

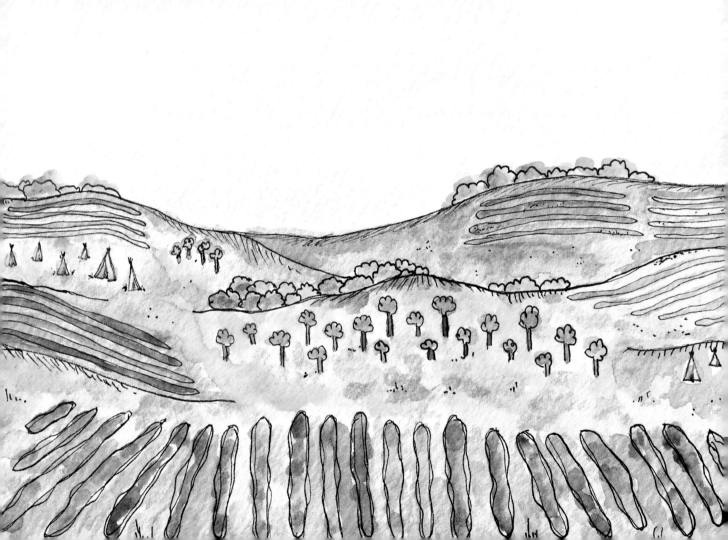

I am as Unique as the Clouds.

I am as Simple as
the Grass,

and I am as Deep as the Ocean.

I am as Beautiful as a Flower...

A Wild Flower.

And I am as
Grounded as the
Roots beneath
my Feet.

I am the Earth,

And the Earth is Me.

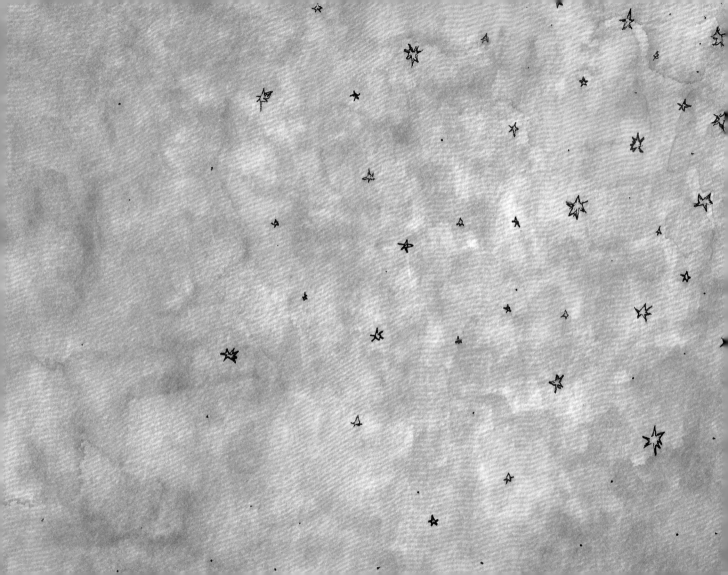

EVERYTHING
IS
CONNECTED

We share our humanity.

Printed on 30% recycled content, 30% post-consumer waste, processed chlorine-free paper by greenerprinter.com

First Stillwater River Publications Edition

ISBN: 978-1-950339-94-5

1 2 3 4 5 6 7 8 9 10

Written & illustrated by Hanna Gerlach. Published by Stillwater River Publications, Pawtucket, RI, USA.

Publisher's Cataloging-In-Publication Data (Prepared by The Donohue Group, Inc.)

Names: Gerlach, Hanna, author, illustrator.

Title: I am the Earth, and the Earth is me / by Hanna Gerlach.

Description: First Stillwater River Publications edition. | Pawtucket, RI, USA : Stillwater River Publications, [2020] | Interest age level: 007-012.

Identifiers: ISBN 9781950339945

Subjects: LCSH: Nature--Juvenile fiction. | Self-esteem in children--Juvenile fiction. | Environmental responsibility--Juvenile fiction. | CYAC: Nature--Fiction. | Self-esteem--Fiction. | Environmental responsibility--Fiction.

Classification: LCC PZ7.1.G4748 Ia 2020 | DDC [E]--dc23